THE MOST
BEAUTIFUL TREE

MELODY CARLSON
ILLUSTRATIONS BY DONNA RACE

HARVEST HOUSE PUBLISHERS
Eugene, Oregon

THE MOST BEAUTIFUL TREE

Text Copyright © 2001 by Melody Carlson
Published by Harvest House Publishers
Eugene, Oregon 97402

Library of Congress Cataloging-in-Publication Data

Carlson, Melody.
    The most beautiful tree / Melody Carlson ; illustrations by Donna Race.
        p. cm.
    Summary: A tree that has bragged about being the most beautiful in
the forest becomes a Christmas tree fit for a king, but a barefoot little boy
named Leo helps him find the inner beauty that comes from giving.
    ISBN 0-7369-0437-9
    [1. Christmas trees--Fiction. 2. Generosity--Fiction. 3. Christmas--
Fiction. 4. Stories in rhyme.] I. Race, Donna, ill. II. Title.

PZ8.3.C214 Mo 2001
[E]--dc21

Design and Production by Garborg Design Works,
Minneapolis, Minnesota

Scripture quotations are from the New King James Version. Copyright © 1982 by Thomas Nelson,
Inc. Used by permission. All rights reserved.

Printed in Hong Kong

01 02 03 04 05 06 07 08 09 10 / NG / 10 9 8 7 6 5 4 3 2 1

Beyond the valley and high on a hill
  Stands a small forest, green and still.
Happy trees grow there; they belong to the king.
Sometimes you can even hear them sing.

Each day they grow taller—wide, and strong,
Waiting for Christmas, now it won't be long
Until the royal woodsmen come search for a tree
For the town's square—*now who will it be?*

Only the biggest, the strongest, the best
  Will be selected, removed from the rest.
  And carried in triumph to the valley below,
To stand in the village, to shimmer and glow.

aid Matilda, the short pine,
        to a hemlock named Bruce,
"Do you think they might choose
    big Samson the Spruce?
Or maybe Augustus; he's a great noble fir.
Or perhaps Holly Berry—you can never be sure."

"Pish-posh!" said a pine tree, his name Thaddeus.
"It's quite plain to see who's best among us."
He stretched straight and tall,
    his branches held wide,
And continued to speak,
    his words filled with pride:

"*I* am the finest, the grandest, the best.
The most beautiful tree, from the east to the west.
And those silly woodcutters surely will see,
If they want the best,
    they can only pick me!"

he other trees rumbled
      and grumbled and said,
"For a nice-looking tree, you've sure got a big head!"
"You're jealous," said Thaddeus, "but just wait and see
Who the woodcutters pick for the most beautiful tree."

Then he paused for a moment to listen below.
"I now hear them coming, and soon I will go.
I'll think of you trees, when I'm down in the square
All wrapped in fine tinsel with hardly a care."

The woodcutters sang as they climbed up the hill.
"We'll hunt and we'll search forever until
We find the best tree—the tallest, the straightest,
The biggest, the greenest, the finest, the greatest!"

ow the trees all grew quiet,
             standing straight and tall
As the woodcutters walked and inspected them all.
And at last they stopped, and there they stood
Before the tree they thought would be good.

"This is it," they proclaimed. "It's the one, it's the best.
It's taller and straighter than all of the rest."
And Thaddeus grinned, just bursting with pride,
As he stretched out his branches from side to side.

Ker-whack went the ax right into his trunk.
It hurt quite a lot—then he fell down *ker-plunk!*
This couldn't be how it was meant to be.
Was this how you treat the most beautiful tree?

e looked up at the trees as he lay on the ground.
Humbled and helpless, he made not a sound.
The woodcutters loaded him onto a sled,
As he slid down the hill, he trembled with dread.

When they came to the valley, they slowed to a walk.
And that's when the woodcutters started to talk.
"Our Christmas will be rather bleak for this year…
There's no fatted goose; only baked beans, I fear…"

"The crops were so bad, there's no money for toys…
A pitiful Christmas for our girls and our boys…"
"But at least we will have this beautiful tree
For all to enjoy—so lovely to see."

t took sixteen men just to raise him up straight.
But once he was standing, he looked really great!
People paused from their work and stopped to admire.
"What a beautiful tree! None's ever been higher!"

Then came a large crew with boxes and ladders,
And brightly jeweled baubles piled high upon platters.
Fine silver and gold pretty ornamentations
Far beyond Thaddeus's best expectations.

The tinsel was heavy, the garlands great lengths,
But Thaddeus held them all up with his strength.
Determined to be the best Christmas tree yet,
No tree could be finer—on that he would bet!

nd there stood Thaddeus—in center square
For people to come, to awe, and to stare,
To oggle and boggle, to soak in and savor.
Then quickly they turned and returned to their labor.

But one barefooted boy, too little for work,
Stayed with the tree and played in the dirt.
Thaddeus first wanted to shoo him away.
But after awhile, he asked him to stay.

The lad's name was Leo
and he wasn't half bad.
Although very poor,
he never seemed sad.
For hours on end,
he chatted with cheer,
And Thaddeus liked
to have the boy near.

ut one frosty morning,
           snow covered the street,
And Thaddeus looked down at young Leo's bare feet.
"Where are you shoes?" hc asked. "Aren't you cold?"
"We've no money," shrugged Leo. "That's all I am told."

Thaddeus gazed down at his branches adorned.
He felt sad and confused and a little forlorn.
He shook loose a bauble from the tip of a bough,
Made of fine silver and shaped like a cow.

"Here, Leo," he said. "Take this and go find
A pair of warm shoes that will treat your feet kind."
Leo blinked as he picked up the valuable toy.
"Thank you, dear Thaddeus,"
    he cried out with joy.

he next day Leo came, but his feet were still bare.
"Where are your new shoes?" asked Thaddeus. *"Where?"*
"I'm sorry," said Leo. "But old Widow Edison
Was so very sick, she needed some medicine.

"My feet may be cold, but I can get by.
Without medicine, the poor woman would die."
"I see," said Thaddeus as he shook off a gold goose.
"Here, Leo, now take this, and go get some shoes!"

Young Leo shot off, as fast as he dare.
And Thaddeus looked down at his branch slightly bare.
"Surely, no one will notice what's missing from me.
They'll continue to think I'm a beautiful tree."

hen Leo came back he *still* had no shoes.
"Don't worry," he said, "I've got some great news.
That goose came in handy—it really was good.
It bought a poor family a whole lot of food!"

"But what about *you?* What about your bare feet?"
Leo shrugged. "It's okay. At least I can eat."
Thaddeus gazed at his riches, the silver and gold,
Then to Leo's feet, now blue from the cold.

"This is simply not right, it's simply unjust.
Someone must do something. *Somebody must!*
Come, Leo, come now in my branches and climb.
Come fill up your pockets with all you can find!"

or the rest of the day, young Leo climbed high.
It seemed the tree's branches reached clear to the sky.
Then down he would come, with fat bulging pockets,
And race through town, just like a fast rocket!

And with the poor people, these fine gifts he shared.
The townsfolk all cried—*at last someone cared!*
It seemed that their Christmas would not be so bad.
For Thaddeus the tree had made them all glad.

Just seeing their faces made him happy too.
And at last little Leo wore shoes that looked new!
Sure, Thaddeus saw that his branches were bare,
But strangely enough, he just didn't care.

hen Leo came back he *still* had no shoes.
"Don't worry," he said, "I've got some great news.
That goose came in handy—it really was good.
It bought a poor family a whole lot of food!"

"But what about *you?* What about your bare feet?"
Leo shrugged. "It's okay. At least I can eat."
Thaddeus gazed at his riches, the silver and gold,
Then to Leo's feet, now blue from the cold.

"This is simply not right, it's simply unjust.
Someone must do something. *Somebody must!*
Come, Leo, come now in my branches and climb.
Come fill up your pockets with all you can find!"

or the rest of the day, young Leo climbed high.
It seemed the tree's branches reached clear to the sky.
Then down he would come, with fat bulging pockets,
And race through town, just like a fast rocket!

And with the poor people, these fine gifts he shared.
The townsfolk all cried—*at last someone cared!*
It seemed that their Christmas would not be so bad.
For Thaddeus the tree had made them all glad.

Just seeing their faces made him happy too.
And at last little Leo wore shoes that looked new!
Sure, Thaddeus saw that his branches were bare,
But strangely enough, he just didn't care.

oor Thaddeus now understood his condition
Was not very lovely—a sorry rendition
Of what the king's tree was expected to be
For he no longer was the most beautiful tree.

Just then he was startled by loud trumpet blasts
And clattering hooves that thundered right past.
But all of the horses stopped dead in the square,
And men in fine uniforms looked up to stare.

One climbed from his horse
    and gaped up at the tree,
"Just what kind of joke
    is this s'posed to be?"
The others agreed,
    saying things just as mean,
Like, "This is the ugliest tree
    that I've seen!"

oor Thaddeus, embarrassed, just wanted to hide.
Never again would he puff with pride.
The soldiers declared: "This tree will not do!
Let's throw it away and get one that is new.

"Our king has been gone for nearly a year—
Just what'll he think when he finally gets here?"
Thaddeus knew that it didn't look good.
"Come!" said the leader. "Let's make firewood!"

But that's when the townsfolk rallied about,
Led by young Leo, they started to shout.
"Don't touch him!" they cried.
    "We demand that you halt!
For he's good and we love him—
    it's not the tree's fault!"

he fussing and fighting went on for an hour,
While Thaddeus watched without any power.
He feared that today he'd make history lore—
For the ugliest tree, and the first Christmas war.

And just when he thought that the battle was lost
He saw a fine caravan coming across
The village square—heading straight for the crowd!
No one else noticed; they were yelling too loud.

The royal coach stopped and the crowd turned to see
The king stepping out, not far from the tree.
And like a great wave, the townsfolk bowed down
To honor their king—who'd come back to town.

reetings!" called the king. "Too long I've been gone."
He looked at the crowd then asked, "What is wrong?"
The leader stepped forward and fell to one knee,
"Your Highness, we meant to get rid of this tree."

Thaddeus felt the king's gaze fall on him,
All shabby and tattered—with a broken limb.
"This tree's a disgrace," said the king. "It can't stay.
Go on and remove it—just take it away!"

"Stop!" declared Leo. And then he stepped up.
A soldier growled loudly, "Get back there, young pup!"
    "Hush!" said the king. "Dear child, have no fear.
    What can you tell me that I need to hear?"

oung Leo bowed down, then quietly spoke,
"Your people were needy and hungry and broke.
We had a bad year, the crops got no rain.
Your people were hurting, some even in pain.

"We'd almost forgotten what the season's about.
But the tree stripped his branches to help us all out.
And if it was wrong, then just blame it on me.
But, dear king, I beg you—*please, don't hurt the tree!*"

The king nodded sadly. "If only I'd known
How badly you suffered—I would've raced home.
How thankful I am that this tree wisely shared
The wealth of my ornaments
   —*how great that he cared!*"

haddeus was spared when the king's voice was raised:
"This tree will remain, his deeds to be praised.
Tomorrow is Christmas, we'll gather to sing
Beneath this kind tree, our voices will ring!"

But in the late night, folks came to the tree.
They all tied on items, though so quietly.
And by light of day, *Thaddeus looked grand!*
Adorned with sweet gifts, each one made by hand!

His branches were filled with such wonderful things—
Dollies, and cookies, and birds with real wings.
"This tree," said the king, "has a lesson for living—
A reminder to all: 'tis the season for giving.

"For on the first Christmas, God gave the best gift,
His very own Son—our spirits to lift.
And so," said the king, his voice filled with glee,
"I hereby proclaim—*the most beautiful tree!"*

THE END